At that moment Silver Twitch was trying to walk Gabriel along the plank over the blanket ocean.

It had been a week since Mum had held the getting-to-know-you party for the neighbours. As Stevie watched Eshe dive Gabriel into the blanket ocean, flapping his tail with her fingers, she thought about all the amazing things that had happened.

1. Nanny Blue had come to the party, especially to see her.

2. Stevie had thought Eshe was going to be mean.

3. Nanny Blue had fallen and Eshe had helped her.

4. Stevie and Eshe had spent the following week becoming *very best friends*.

Also, they'd managed to convince their parents it would be a good idea for them to have their first sleepover, and tonight was the night. Both girls were ridiculously excited. Stevie felt the happiest she'd felt in ages, although she *was* starting to miss her mum.

1. Mum was in Paris for two nights to take photos of a famous orchestra.

2. Taking photos was Mum's job. She was really good at it.

3. Mum had put a big heart around the date on the calendar in the kitchen to show Stevie two nights wasn't very long at all.

4. Stevie hadn't really wanted Mum to go.

Stevie's mum had left her a little note on blue notepaper. Stevie had folded it neatly and put it in her pocket. It said:

Dear Stevie,
Have a lovely time when I'm away and have fun with your dad.
I love you very much. I am so lucky to be your mum. Don't forget the blackbirds xxxx

Stevie had no intention of forgetting the blackbirds. For the past few weeks, from just after they'd first moved in, Stevie and Mum had been watching a blackbird come and go to a nest inside the thick hedge that ran alongside the garden. Even though the nest was well hidden, Stevie and Mum had investigated, and found a way to watch the nest through a gap in the leaves. For two weeks the female blackbird had been sitting on a clutch of eggs, while the male bird flew back and forth with worms for her to eat. Whilst Stevie was not going to disturb them, or touch them (Mum had explained very carefully that touching birds' nests put the chicks in danger) she was going to make sure they were okay while Mum was away. Part of her hoped the chicks would hatch soon, but maybe *not* before Mum got home.

And Stevie *was* having a lovely time.
Last night Stevie and Dad had stayed
up late watching movies, and now he
was in the kitchen making salami
sandwiches and cutting apple stars.

Dad's husband Stuart would be
arriving any minute. He'd had to work
in the dairy yesterday, but had promised
they'd spend today all together.

"Walk the plank! Walk the plank!" shouted Eshe, hopping Silver along behind Fig on the plank made of lolly sticks.

Stevie came out of her daydream.

"Noooo!" she said in a silly voice, making Fig shake, his little tail nearly sliding off.

"You've not heard the last of me!" Eshe said, putting Silver down.

Stevie handed Fig to her, then picked up Daddy Gabriel. "*En garde*!" she said, putting on her best pirate voice and holding his home-made cutlass straight

up in front
of him.

Soon the
two girls
were laughing,
battling with
Gabriel and
Fig on the
blanket, the teacup house and its
contents spread out in front of them.

Just then there was a loud
"**Woof!**" from the far end of the
garden. Once, twice, three times.

"Woof! Woof! Woof!"

"Rio!" said Stevie excitedly, jumping up.

"Who's Rio?" said Eshe.

"I forgot to tell you about Dad and Stuart's puppy!" said Stevie. "She's a rescued Labradoodle. The silliest, curliest, cuddliest dog you'll ever meet! I haven't seen her since we moved. Come on!"

Stevie popped Gabriel in her pocket, and Eshe took Fig. Together they ran down the garden, ready to make a big fuss of their puppy visitor.

From where they sat in the girls'
pockets, Gabriel and Fig Twitch
could see:

1. A **BIG** dog entering the
   garden.
2. The look of fear on Mama Bo
   and Silver's faces as it headed
   in their direction.

The dog was bouncing and barking
and that meant only one thing.
Trouble!

Chapter Two
Woof and Roll

"Silver," said Mama Bo in a very calm voice. "I need you to listen to me very carefully."

Silver sat still and looked at her mum. It wasn't often Mama Bo sounded this serious.

"**Woof!**" said the dog from the far end of the garden.

"What are we going to do,

Mama?" asked Silver.

"The dog is very **big**," said Mama Bo. "If it comes anywhere near us, we're in trouble. We're going to have to keep our eyes open. And whatever you do, don't go anywhere near its mouth. I wish we weren't on the ground down here. I'd feel much better about all this if we were upstairs on the desk in Stevie's room, like usual."

Silver nodded. For once, she didn't feel adventurous or full of ideas. She just wanted to keep safe and was ready to do whatever her mama told her.

"**Woof! Woof!**" said the dog.

Mama Bo and Silver gave each other a worried look and Silver reached over to give her mum a huggle. They didn't like the sound of this, not one bit.

Stuart was at the far end of the garden, holding a lead attached to the bouncing puppy in one hand, and a pair of bright blue roller skates with a rainbow stripe in the other. He led Rio along the grass to where Stevie and Eshe were rushing towards him.

"Stevie!" he said happily. "It's so good to see you!"

"And you!" said Stevie, giving him the biggest hug as Rio jumped up and down excitedly at her feet. "This is Eshe, she's my best friend. She's sleeping over tonight.

Did Dad tell you about the blackbird nest? You can spot it really well from here – look!"

Stevie pointed to the gap in the hedge further along the garden. "There are two of them. One of them is sitting on some eggs!" Stevie was talking very fast and was bouncing almost as much as the puppy.

"Wonderful!" said Stuart, peering to where Stevie had pointed. "We'll make sure Rio doesn't disturb them. Hello, Eshe. Pleased to meet you!"

"Pleased to meet you, too," said Eshe. "Hello, girl!" she said, kneeling down to rub the fur on Rio's forehead.

"Pleased to meet you."

"Woof! Woof! Woof!"

Rio jumped up enthusiastically. Stuart loosened the lead and spoke to her in a gentle, firm voice.

"Now, Rio," said Stuart in a serious voice. "Sit!"

Rio did not sit. Rio bounced up and down.

"Rio..." said Stuart very seriously indeed. "Sit!"

"Is that what you call puppy training?" giggled Stevie.

"I don't understand," said Stuart, although he was still smiling. "I've been doing all the things the puppy trainer said I should and practising all the time. She only seems to do what I say when there's nobody around to see it!"

Stevie and Eshe giggled.

"We could help you train her!" said Stevie and Eshe at the same time.

"Sit!"
said Stevie in
a serious voice.

"Sit!"
said Eshe in
an even more
serious voice.

"Woof!"
barked Rio,
bouncing up
and down.

"We'll get there," said Stuart. "Anyway, these are for you." He handed Stevie the beautiful pair of blue roller skates and she looked at them wide-eyed.

"They are?"

"Your dad said you were thinking about getting some. These were my nephew's, but he's grown out of them now. They're yours. If you want them."

"Want them?" said Stevie excitedly. "You can say that again. Thank you so much!" She waggled them at Eshe. "Do you fancy a skate?" Eshe always took her green roller skates with her everywhere.

Stevie turned to her dad. "Will you take us up The Lane, so we can practise. Please? Can you?"

Dad nodded. The Lane was a long path, too small for cars, and used by local children and their grown-ups when they wanted to learn to ride their bikes. It would be perfect for roller skating, as it was nowhere near the road. "It will give Stu and Rio a chance to settle in."

"Yes!" said Stevie, as she and Eshe ran inside to get Eshe's skates. It was turning into a brilliant day.

Chapter Three
A Bounce Too Far

Gabriel Twitch poked his head out
of Stevie's pocket. The world was
bobbing up and down, side to side,
and he could feel his body juddering
because of Stevie's uncertain skating.
He looked across to Eshe, who was
in front of Stevie, and actually, very
neatly and very smoothly, skating
backwards so she could encourage
her friend. From the pocket in Eshe's

dress, two little ears and an excited face were poking out. Daddy Gabriel bet Fig was having the time of his life. It must feel very different to be in the pocket of somebody who was so good at skating.

Bump! Wobble! Bump! went Stevie. No such luck for Daddy Gabriel, who was starting to feel a bit travel sick.

Daddy Gabriel was right. Fig *was* having the time of his life

He felt the breeze rush past his face as Eshe did balletic swishes with her legs, and he whizzed along, taking in all the wildlife, the trees and sights of spring.

Daffodils bobbed their trumpets.
Birds chirruped. It was easy to think
all was right with the world.

But it wasn't.

Both rabbits

only hoped Silver

and Mama Bo were safe, with that
over-enthusiastic puppy on the loose…

Stevie wobbled down The Lane in her
new skates, holding tightly onto Dad's
hand. Eshe was skating with ease in
front of them, but she'd had roller
skates for over a year. Stevie tried to
copy what her friend was doing, but
this was going to take practice. She
held onto Dad's arm tightly as one leg
went in one direction and the other
went in a completely different one.

"Arggh," she said in frustration. "I'll never be able to do this!"

"Yes you will," said Eshe. "First time I went on skates properly I fell in a puddle and had to walk around for the rest of the morning with a wet bottom."

"Well, we'll try and avoid that," said Dad.

Stevie held onto his arm more tightly. Skating was really *hard!*

She pulled her concentration face, the one everyone said made her look like her mum.

She was going to practise skating
every day until she was really good
at it.

Back at the cottage, Stuart thought
that if he let Rio have a run around
in the garden, it might get some of
her energy out before the others
got back.

It all happened so fast.

Stuart let Rio, now the most excitable puppy in the universe, off her lead and into the garden. He smiled as she ran about. The garden was very secure, so he wasn't worried about her escaping, and he'd chase after her if she started

Bounce...

bounce...

bounce...

to eat any of the plants – he knew how important they were to Stevie. But, he didn't spot the teacup house at all.

Bounce, bounce, bounce, bounce,

went Rio along the garden.

Rio stopped. She was on the blanket. She was right in front of the teacup house, sniffing, sniffing, and…

Silver and Mama Bo watched in horror from the blanket, as the dog pushed her **big** wet face into their home.

The whole teacup house toppled, and with it, all their little Twitch things.

Rio went on, sniffing and snuffling *inside* the upturned house. **Over** went the Twitches' beds. **Over** went Silver and Fig's toy box, scattering all their tiny toys across the picnic blanket.

The pots from the kitchen went flying too, and a big frying pan.

Over went the coffee table, all the little cushions, the dining chair and even the bookcase with all the little books. A copy of *The Hoppit* landed right in front of the two Twitches' feet.

Mama Bo and Silver stood, frozen to the spot. They held paws very tightly.

It felt as if it was only a matter of moments before the dog spotted them, and then they'd be done for. Neither of them fancied being chewed on like a juicy bone. Mama Bo looked at Silver. Silver looked at Mama Bo.

"Run!" shouted Mama Bo. "Run for your life!"

She pulled Silver with her, and they both began to run as fast as their little legs could carry them, across the blanket and away from the dog's big paws.

Rio, who'd spotted them now, began to bound after them, fast and panting. They had no idea where they were going, but all they knew was that if they didn't get away from Rio as quickly as possible, there was every chance they'd end up as a dog's dinner!

Chapter Four
Into the Hedge

Mama Bo and Silver ran and ran, as fast as they could, right across the garden and into the hedge. Looking over her shoulder, Silver could see Rio's big open mouth and big bouncing paws getting nearer and nearer.

"There's only one thing for it," she said to Mama Bo. "We need to climb up the hedge and hide inside it!"

The two rabbits looked up at the hedge.

It was dark and scary,
with all sorts of spiky
leaves, and pointy twigs
and hidden things. Silver
was sure she could see
some wisps of
spiderweb…

But there was no time to think about it. They had no choice. Just as Rio dived at them, with her mouth open and her tongue out, they scurried into the roots of the hedge…

On The Lane, Stevie was getting the hang of roller skating. She was starting to use the skates in long sweeps, each foot almost gliding past the other, and she could nearly skate by herself now.

"I'll be showing you how to do this next!" said Eshe, doing a complete spin

and a fancy stop. She did a little bow
and Stevie laughed.

"Not quite…but one day!"

"You're making me want to try,"
said Dad. "Maybe we can convince
Stuart that it would be a good idea for
us all to have a pair of skates."

"Yes!" said Eshe and Stevie at the
same time.

"Magpie!" yelled Eshe, all of a
sudden, as a big black and white bird
flew past their heads in the direction of
the cottage. It stopped on a nearby tree.

"Aren't we supposed to salute them?" said Stevie.

"Or say 'one for sorrow, two for joy'…or something?" said Eshe.

"Ah, I don't believe in all that superstition," said Dad, helping Stevie let go of his arm so she could try skating all by herself. "How much trouble can one bird bring?'"

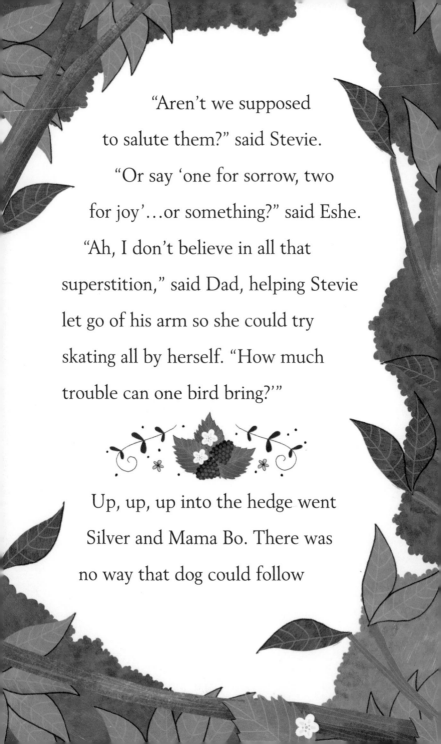

Up, up, up into the hedge went Silver and Mama Bo. There was no way that dog could follow

them – the
hedge was thick
with leaves
and twigs.

"I think we can stop now," said Mama Bo.

"I think so too," said Silver.

They sat on a branch, underneath a particularly thick cluster of twigs. The two rabbits didn't say anything for a moment, both of them taking deep breaths, relieved to be safe. That had been close!

"We made it!" laughed Mama Bo, eventually.

"We did!" said Silver, putting her paws around her mama for another huggle. She loved adventures, but this one had been quite terrifying. And it wasn't over yet.

Now they
were in the
hedge with
no easy way
back home.

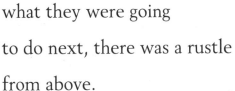

Just as the
two rabbits
were planning
what they were going
to do next, there was a rustle
from above.

"What was that?" said Mama Bo.

"I don't know..." said Silver, as they

heard the sound again. There was a

rustle, then a **bump**, then a rustle,

and a scratching sound. It was coming from directly above their heads.

The two rabbits looked up.

The cluster of twigs was moving about and little pieces of grass and twig were

dropping

down

onto

them.

Something was above them, shaking...

"Mama," said Silver slowly. "I think we're sitting underneath *a nest*!"

Just as Silver said these words, something shadowy jumped down onto the branch beside them, and the two rabbits were confronted by a pair of bright eyes, looking directly at them...

Chapter Five
What a Mess!

By the time Stuart realized his mistake,
it was too late.

"Rio! Rio! Here, girl!" he called.
The puppy ran back towards him and
let him attach the lead to her collar.
She was totally unaware of the
mayhem she'd caused, and was panting
happily. He tied the lead to a tree,
patted her soft head, and rushed over
to what he now saw was the teacup

house, totally knocked over with its
contents spilled out everywhere.

"Oh no," said Stuart, not knowing
where to start. He lifted the teacup
house from the blanket, and carried
it carefully over to the garden table.

He then went back and started to
pick up the little Twitch bits and
pieces that had been scattered
everywhere. This would take
some time...

Hmm, I'll need a wet cloth, soapy water, some tissue, and maybe some furniture polish, he thought, as he undid Rio's lead and took her into the kitchen.

Stevie was skating back to the cottage along The Lane. She'd got it! She'd finally got it! It was true she couldn't stop very easily. It was true that she still wobbled a bit. But, for one brilliant moment, she skated along the path, without holding onto her dad, and felt the breeze through her hair and the absolute excitement of

being able to do something she'd
wanted to do for so long.

"That's it!" said Dad
enthusiastically as they reached the
garden gate.

"Yes!" cried Eshe. "Go, Stevie!"

"I'm doing it!" she called
out, feeling like the
happiest person
in the world.

"I can't wait
to show Stuart!
And Mum
when she's
back!"

Dad reached out to help her stop, and she twirled about at his feet, nearly landing with a crash, but going *puff!* into his tummy instead. It didn't matter. She had skated, by herself, even if it was for just a few minutes.

As the three of them entered the garden it was Eshe who looked up and saw the teacup house first.

"Um, Stevie," she said. The teacup house was standing on the table where Stuart had left it, but most of the contents were still strewn about the blanket and lawn, in a total mess.

Stevie's heart dropped. She ran towards it, forgetting she was on her skates, and fell down with a **bump.**

Suddenly, it was all too much for Stevie. "Daaaaaaad!" she cried.

Dad kneeled down beside her and helped her take off her skates.

Eshe ran on tiptoes, still in hers, to the blanket and started picking up Twitch furniture, looking to see if anything was broken. Stevie finally pulled off both skates and

ran over to the teacup house, checking it for damage, running her fingers over all the pretty details to feel for chips or dents, or worse. Dad was close behind.

"Oh Stevie," he said, putting his arms out to give her a hug.

"What happened?" Stevie asked.

"A puppy," said Dad, slowly.

"You wouldn't think a dog could cause all this mess in such a short time," said Eshe. "But I don't think anything's broken."

Stevie had a tight feeling in her chest as she pulled Gabriel Twitch out from her pocket. He was perfect, just as he should be. Eshe pulled out Fig from her own pocket, and the two girls

looked at each other, looked at the
blanket, and then back at each other.

"Where are Silver and Bo?" said
Stevie.

"They must be here somewhere,"
said Eshe, feeling about on the blanket
and the grass nearby. But she didn't
sound very sure.

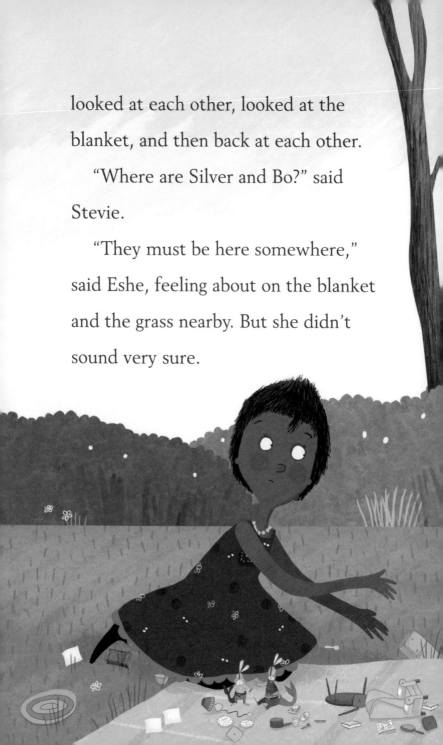

The two girls started looking for the mummy and daughter rabbits immediately. Soggy books, a coffee table with a missing leg, a muddy little patchwork bedspread…but no Silver, and no Bo.

"What if Rio's eaten them?" said Stevie. "What are we going to do?"

Eshe put her arm around Stevie as she started to cry – just as Stuart came back into the garden with the cleaning equipment. Realizing it was too late to make everything all right, he and Dad looked at each other sadly.

Gabriel and Fig Twitch were unable to move or do anything. The sight of all their beautiful things, soggy and strewn about, filled them with despair. But that was nothing compared to Mama Bo and Silver

being missing, maybe eaten by the
dog! It was enough to send both
rabbits into shakes of fear. What if
Mama Bo and Silver never came
home?

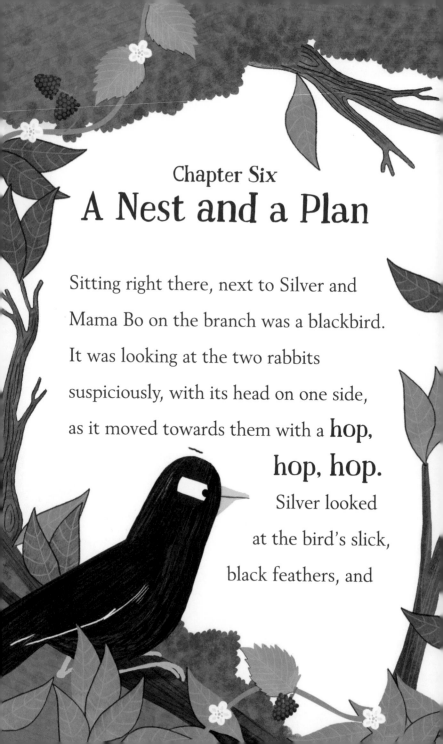

Chapter Six
A Nest and a Plan

Sitting right there, next to Silver and
Mama Bo on the branch was a blackbird.
It was looking at the two rabbits
suspiciously, with its head on one side,
as it moved towards them with a hop,
hop, hop.
Silver looked
at the bird's slick,
black feathers, and

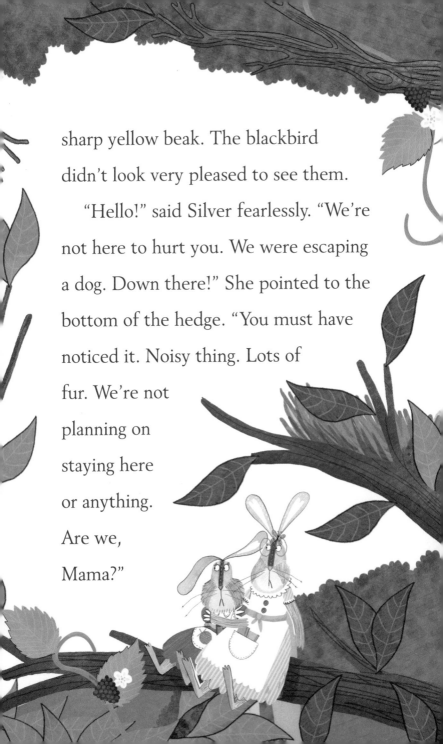

sharp yellow beak. The blackbird
didn't look very pleased to see them.

"Hello!" said Silver fearlessly. "We're
not here to hurt you. We were escaping
a dog. Down there!" She pointed to the
bottom of the hedge. "You must have
noticed it. Noisy thing. Lots of
fur. We're not
planning on
staying here
or anything.
Are we,
Mama?"

Mama Bo shook her head slowly. "No," she said. "In fact, if you've got any ideas on the best way for us to get home without having to go on the ground again and risk being gobbled up by that dog, we'd be most grateful…"

The blackbird continued to stare and **hop** nearer to the two rabbits. It looked up

at its nest, then back
at the rabbits, and
then out
through the
gap in the hedge.
It was shaking its
head and stamping one of
its little clawed feet.

"There's something wrong," said
Silver to her mother.

"There is," said Mama Bo. "But
what? What is it, Mr Blackbird? What's
wrong? Can we help you?"

The blackbird looked at them,
almost as though the softness of their

voices had calmed him down, and he understood that they really didn't mean him any harm. But then there was a wild scratching noise, a flutter and a flap, and the thick hedge in front of them started to shudder. It was then Silver realized the blackbird was afraid. He spread out his wings, almost as though he was trying to protect something.

"What is it?" asked Silver gently. "What's wrong?"

Suddenly, a big beak started pushing through the gaps in the hedge. There came a strange sound like a baby's rattle being shaken – it was a bird's call. Then suddenly, Mama Bo and Silver came face to face with the very fierce and very determined, black and white feathered head of a magpie.

In the garden, Stevie and Eshe put Gabriel and Fig Twitch, plus all their rescued belongings, inside the teacup house. Then she, Eshe, Dad and Stuart began combing the garden for the missing Silver and Mama Bo. Stevie was so upset about the Twitches that she had forgotten all about the blackbirds. Maybe that's why she didn't notice the big magpie perched on the hedge, and pushing its head right inside the blackbirds' nesting place...

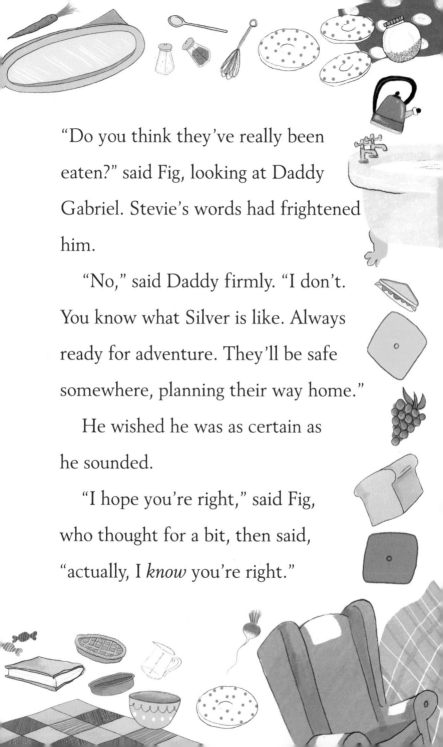

"Do you think they've really been eaten?" said Fig, looking at Daddy Gabriel. Stevie's words had frightened him.

"No," said Daddy firmly. "I don't. You know what Silver is like. Always ready for adventure. They'll be safe somewhere, planning their way home."

He wished he was as certain as he sounded.

"I hope you're right," said Fig, who thought for a bit, then said, "actually, I *know* you're right."

He puffed out his little chest.

"You know," said Fig, "I think we should start sorting this stuff out. We could get this place spick and span in no time."

"Good plan," said Daddy Gabriel.

"Although, don't you think Stevie will notice?"

"I think she'll be too busy to notice, and we could leave out a few obvious dirty things, just enough to make her uncertain…"

"That," said Daddy Gabriel, rolling up his sleeves and patting his son on the head, "is an **excellent** idea."

Then he began to heave and push things back into position, while Fig headed off to the little Twitch kitchen to find a mop and some rubber gloves, trying very hard not to think about what might have happened to Mama Bo and Silver.

Chapter Seven
Up, Up and Away

Silver didn't have time to be scared.
She suddenly understood what
was happening. This blackbird was
protecting its nest, because the magpie
was trying to get to it. She and Mama
Bo needed to do something to help
and they needed to do it quickly. The
thick leaves and prickles of the hedge
wouldn't fend off the magpie for long.

"We need to make it go away!" said

Silver to Mama Bo. "We need to scare the magpie away!" Silver looked about her, then closed her eyes and imagined what it was she needed...

She needed to make the magpie think there was another really big bird hiding in the hedge. She needed to make the magpie think *it* was in danger.

"I've got it!" she said to Mama Bo, out of breath and excited. "We've got no time to waste. We shall make a scaremagpie!"

"A what?" said Mama Bo.

"A scaremagpie!" said Silver. "Like a

scarecrow…but a **big** bird, *more scary* than a magpie, that'll send it away so it doesn't come back!"

Mama Bo thought her daughter really was very clever indeed. Soon, she was holding a bunch of sticks, some big leaves, and some coils of honeysuckle bundled together to make some wings.

Silver rolled up a bunch of leaves to make a big ball, that could almost be mistaken for a head, and she made a beak out of two curled leaves. Then taking both of their mermaid tails, the Twitches tied each of them up into a ball to make two, bright eyes.

The blackbird seemed to agree this was a good idea, and quickly helped them to build the scaremagpie.

"Cawww! Cawwww!" shouted Silver and Mama Bo, flapping the scaremagpie's wings, which they moved with sticks like a puppet.

"Cawww! Cawww!"

Their pretend bird made a lot of flapping, and a lot of noise. They jostled it, and rustled it, and poked its beak in the direction of the magpie.

There was a bit of a kerfuffle. The magpie pecked in, and in, but the Twitches didn't give up.

"We need to flap harder!" said Silver.

"Right ho!" said Mama Bo, furiously moving her stick up and down and calling out "Cawwww!" with all her might.

Suddenly, the magpie's rustling and pecking stopped. Silver caught its shining eye through a gap in the leaves, and she knew it was afraid. The magpie made

one last rattling sound, one last rustle
of the hedge, a few flaps of its wings,
and then it was gone.

"Ha!"
Silver said.

"Ha!" said
Mama Bo.

"**Tweet,
whistle,
whoop,**"

said the blackbird, who was hopping
up and down. He looked very happy
indeed. Then he reached out a wing,
scooped up Mama Bo and Silver, and
lifted them up onto the higher branch.

There, settled deep in the warmth
and thickness of the nest, was another
blackbird. And this one was sitting
beside four pale blue-green and red
speckled eggs.

"Mama!" cried Silver in awe.
"There they are!"

And then they heard a sound.

Tap tap. Tap tap tap. Tap.

Soft, peach, afternoon sunlight shone through the gaps in the leaves of the hedge, and the nest was full of golden warmth.

Tap tap. Tap tap tap. Tap.

What was that sound?

The baby birds were hatching!

The mummy blackbird nodded her head at the two Twitches and they both knew she was saying thank you.

"You're most welcome!" said Silver and Mama Bo together. "You're most welcome indeed!"

The daddy blackbird hopped towards them. It was time for them to go. The blackbirds needed space to hatch.

Mama Bo peered out of the hedge to check if the coast was clear, and spotted the teacup house. It was no

longer on the
blanket on
the grass,
but high
up on the
garden
table.

Suddenly, she had an idea.

"I hope you don't mind me
asking," she said to the blackbird,
"but do you think you could help us?
We're trying to avoid a very bouncy
dog. Perhaps you could fly us right
out into the garden, right over to our
teacup house?"

Neither of the rabbits had any idea
if the blackbird knew what Mama Bo
was talking about, but he did bend
down so they could
easily climb onto
his back.

Mama Bo gently pushed her paws
into the black feathers while Silver
clung tightly to her mother's sides.

The daddy blackbird nodded at the mummy blackbird, as tiny corners of beaks and feet began to poke out of the breaking eggshells. Soon the chicks would be fully out, and into the nest.

"Ready?" said Mama Bo to Silver, as she felt the bird about to take off.

"Ready," said Silver, grinning wildly as she wrapped her arms even tighter around Mama Bo.

"Then let's go!" Mama Bo cried. She gave the blackbird's side a soft tap, and he pushed his way through the hedge. Then, they were off – two little toy rabbits on the back of a blackbird,

whoosh...

flying through the early evening air,

their long ears streaming behind them.

And what sights they could see! From

here they could see all the flowers,

the path, bushes and toadstools, not

to mention Stevie and Eshe, Stuart

and Dad, still busily searching for

them at the other end of the garden.

The blackbird flew so fast that, before long, they were almost home. Silver gasped when she saw their teacup house on the garden table.

"Wow, Mama! It looks as good as new again!" exclaimed Silver.

"I knew Stevie would always look after our home," said Mama Bo.

"Here's where we get off, thank you, Mr Blackbird," said Silver and, with that, the bird flew low enough for them to hop off.

"We need to jump!" said Mama Bo. "One, two, three…" Both rabbits closed their eyes at the same time.

Jump!

The two little Twitches fell through the air towards the table. It wasn't too far, but the blackbird hadn't really slowed down very much.

Down,

down...

Silver and Mama Bo landed
with a loud **bump.**

"Perfect landing," Silver
giggled as she realized Mama
Bo had landed upside down
and her little feet were
wiggling in the air.

"Easy for you to say," said Mama Bo, as she turned herself the right way up and gave her daughter a huge squeeze.

Then with all the people in the garden looking for them, they stood perfectly still, waiting to be discovered. What an adventure they'd had! They couldn't wait to see Fig and Daddy Gabriel.

Chapter Eight
Safe and Sound

Several things happened very quickly.

1. Stevie had nearly given up hope.

2. The magpie swooped across

    the garden making all sorts of

    strange sounds.

    3. A male blackbird

    came bursting out

    of the place in

    the hedge where

    the nest was.

4. Stevie spotted something on the garden table, right next to the teacup house.

Standing there, looking a little crumpled, but safe, were Mama Bo and Silver Twitch.

Where had they come from?

How had they got there?

Stevie looked around. Had they been with the furniture all along, and she'd just not seen them in her panic.

"Eshe…" she said slowly. "These weren't here before…were they?"

Eshe ran and stood next to her best friend. She couldn't believe what she was seeing either.

"No...but they're here now...
I wonder where their tails went?"

"I wonder where *they* went!" said
Stevie, suspiciously.

The two girls stared in disbelief as
Dad and Stuart joined them by the
garden table.

"Oh good, you've found them!" said
Stuart. "I really *am* sorry!"

"It wasn't your fault," said Stevie, as
she reunited the two Twitches with the
rest of their family.

Inside, the teacup house looked very
clean and tidy. Yes, there was a pile of
books and some blankets on the floor.

Yes, there was an upside-down
armchair and the contents of the little
toy fridge in a badly stacked pile. Yes,
some of the curtains were hanging off

their poles, and the painting in Mama
Bo and Gabriel's room was on the
wonk, but...Stevie had been *sure* it
was a lot worse than this.

"Well…that's…" She didn't know how to finish her sentence. "Maybe it all seemed so much worse when we first discovered it?" she said.

"Maybe," said Stuart, baffled. An exhausted and sleeping Rio was cuddled up in his arms. She looked far too peaceful to have caused all this mayhem.

"**Tweet, tweet, tweet tweeeet.**" They heard a noise from behind them in the hedge. Stevie couldn't believe it. It couldn't be…

"Shhhh," she said softly.

Everybody gathered quietly by the

gap in the hedge to see what was
happening. They could see the
blackbird family and their chicks – the
babies were properly hatched now, and
the mum and dad blackbirds were
feeding them worms.

"They've hatched!" said Stevie excitedly.

"They really have," said Dad.

"I wish Mum had been here to see them," Stevie said a bit sadly.

"You could call her up and tell her all about it," said Dad. "She'll love that. And you can show her as soon as she gets back tomorrow. Now, why don't you and Eshe go and get into your PJs and I'll make hot chocolate… I'll bring the teacup house upstairs so you can get on with your game."

Stevie peered in the hedge and took one last look at the nest, when

something shimmery caught her eye.
Could it be...?

It looked like one of the Twitches'
mermaid tails! Stevie turned to show
Eshe, but she was already heading back
inside.

"Come on!" Eshe called.

"We need to get these pirate
mermaids back in their ship. We'll make
their tails even better this time, so they
don't fall off again. Are you with me?"

"Aye," said Stevie in her best pirate
mermaid voice. "But I'd rather walk
the plank than call you captain!"

It was getting dark outside and the sky through the teacup house windows was streaked dark blue and bronze. Inside the house, all four Twitches felt so cosy and were so, *so* happy to see each other again.

"As you can see, we did some cleaning up," said Fig, proudly. He was glad to have his mum and his sister home.

"We fought off a magpie with a scaremagpie and flew on the back of a blackbird," said Silver, folding her arms and pulling an "I win" face.

Fig stuck his tongue out at her.

"We went roller skating."

"I'm just glad we're all safe," said
Mama Bo, who'd had more adventure
in one day than she'd had in her
whole life.

"I was thinking…" whispered
Silver when everyone was quiet.
"We really should think about
getting a puppy."

"No way!" the three other Twitches cried out. But they were laughing, warm and safe, and so very glad to be back together again.

Dad brought the hot chocolate into Stevie's room where the two friends were already playing.

"These can be the sea!" said Eshe, flapping out her sheets.

"And the pillows can be the rocks their boat gets stranded on," said Stevie. "I'm going to stay awake ALL night."

"Me too!" said Eshe.

"I heard that!" Dad called, as he left the room, grinning to himself.

Stevie was having so much fun with Eshe! She couldn't wait to see Mum tomorrow, but in the meantime, she felt really, very happy.

Meet the Author

When Hayley Scott was little, she used to make tiny furniture for fairy houses, placing it in scooped out hollows in her back garden. Today, Hayley lives in Norfolk and still loves tiny things. *Teacup House* is her debut series for young readers.

Meet the Illustrator

Pippa Curnick is an illustrator, designer, bookworm and bunny owner. She gets her inspiration from walking in the woods in Derbyshire, where she lives with her partner and their son.

Look out for more Teacup House adventures, coming soon from Hayley and Pippa!

Meet the Twitches
in their very first adventure!

Meet the Twitches,
four tiny toy rabbits who
live inside a Teacup House.

They belong to a girl called Stevie
and she loves playing with them. But
guess what? These toy rabbits have
a secret. They come alive when
Stevie isn't looking!

Open up the Teacup House – and meet
four little rabbit heroes with big ideas!

ISBN 9781474928120
www.usborne.com/fiction

Teacup House

Meet the Twitches

By **Hayley Scott** ❀ Illustrated by **Pippa Curnick**

Join the Twitches
for more fun and mischief!

Stevie and her mum
are having a party, and
have baked an amazing cake.

Stevie's tiny toy rabbits, Silver
and Fig Twitch, decide to bake
a cake too – but they want to use
some of Stevie's yummy icing.
It's time for an adventure...

Open up the Teacup House – and meet
four little rabbit heroes with big ideas!

ISBN 9781474928137
www.usborne.com/fiction

TEACUP HOUSE

The Twitches Bake a Cake

By Hayley Scott ❉ Illustrated by Pippa Curnick

For Nell, always.
And for Aiden, with lots
of love (Hayley)

For two beautiful bunnies
– Primrose & Isabella.
(Pippa)

First published in the UK in 2018 by Usborne Publishing Ltd., Usborne House,
83-85 Saffron Hill, London EC1N 8RT, England. www.usborne.com

Text copyright © Hayley Scott, 2018
The right of Hayley Scott to be identified as the author of this work has been asserted by
her in accordance with the Copyright, Designs and Patents Act, 1988.

Illustrations copyright © Usborne Publishing Ltd., 2018
Illustrations by Pippa Curnick

The name Usborne and the devices ♀♨ are Trade Marks of Usborne Publishing Ltd.

All rights reserved. No part of this publication may be reproduced, stored in a
retrieval system or transmitted in any form or by any means, electronic, mechanical,
photocopying, recording or otherwise without the prior permission of the publisher.
This is a work of fiction. The characters, incidents, and dialogues are products of
the author's imagination and are not to be construed as real. Any resemblance
to actual events or persons, living or dead, is entirely coincidental.

A CIP catalogue record for this book is available from the British Library.

JFMAMJ ASOND/18

ISBN 9781474928144 04367/1
Printed in China.